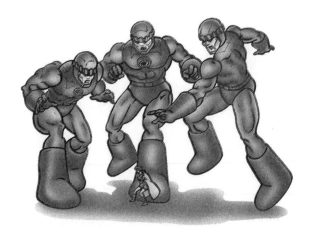

A NOTE TO PARENTS

When your children are ready to "step into reading," giving them the right books—and lots of them—is as crucial as giving them the right food to eat. **Step into Reading Books** present exciting stories and information reinforced with lively, colorful illustrations that make learning to read fun, satisfying, and worthwhile. They are priced so that acquiring an entire library of them is affordable. And they are beginning readers with an important difference—they're written on four levels.

    Step 1 Books, with their very large type and extremely simple vocabulary, have been created for the very youngest readers. **Step 2 Books** are both longer and slightly more difficult. **Step 3 Books,** written to mid-second-grade reading levels, are for the child who has acquired even greater reading skills. **Step 4 Books** offer exciting nonfiction for the increasingly proficient reader.

    Children develop at different ages. **Step into Reading Books,** with their four levels of reading, are designed to help children become good—and interested—readers *faster*. The grade levels assigned to the four steps—preschool through grade 1 for Step 1, grades 1 through 3 for Step 2, grades 2 and 3 for Step 3, and grades 2 through 4 for Step 4—are intended only as guides. Some children move through all four steps very rapi~~""~~ over a period of several years. ~~'~~ child "step into reading" in style.

D1367722

Copyright © 1994 by Marvel Entertainment Group, Inc.. All rights reserved under International
and Pan-American Copyright Conventions. Published in the United States by Random House, Inc.,
New York, and simultaneously in Canada by Random House of Canada Limited, Toronto.

Library of Congress Cataloging-in-Publication Data
Hautzig, Deborah. Battle of the Sentinels / based on teleplays by Mark Edward Edens ; adapted by
Deborah Hautzig ; illustrated by Aristides Ruiz and Josie Yee. p. cm. — (Step into reading. A Step 3
book) At head of title: X-Men. SUMMARY: Jubilee, a mutant teen, learns about her special powers from
a group of other mutants called the X-Men who are fighting robot police called the Sentinels. ISBN 0-
679-86029-0 (pbk) — ISBN 0-679-96029-5 (GLB) [1. Robots—Fiction. 2. Heroes—Fiction. 3. Science
fiction.] I. Edens, Mark Edward. II. Ruiz, Aristides, ill. III. Yee, Josie, ill. IV. Title. V. Series: Step
into reading. Step 3 book. PZ7.H2888Bat 1994 [E]—dc20 93-41361

Manufactured in the United States of America   10 9 8 7 6 5 4 3 2 1
STEP INTO READING is a trademark of Random House, Inc.

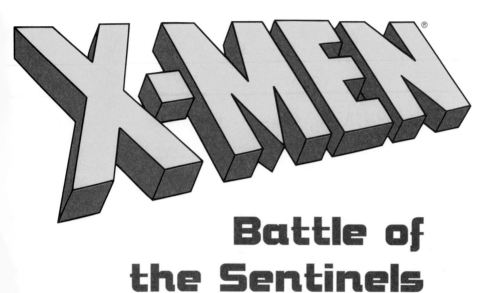

Battle of the Sentinels

based on teleplays by Mark Edward Edens
adapted by Deborah Hautzig
cover illustration by Dana and Del Thompson
illustrated by Aristides Ruiz and Josie Yee

A Step 3 Book

Random House 🏠 New York

1
Mall Madness

Jubilee listened while her foster parents argued downstairs.

"How could you give her name to the Mutant Control Agency?" asked her mother.

"It's for her own safety!" said her father. "Let's hope nobody else finds out that our beautiful Jubilee is a mutant."

Jubilee felt so ashamed!

"Is it my fault that every time I touch a machine, plasmoids shoot out of my fingers and I destroy it?" she said sadly. "I used to be a normal kid!"

Jubilee crept out of the house. As she walked to the mall to sulk, a giant robot called a Sentinel followed her. What was it up to?

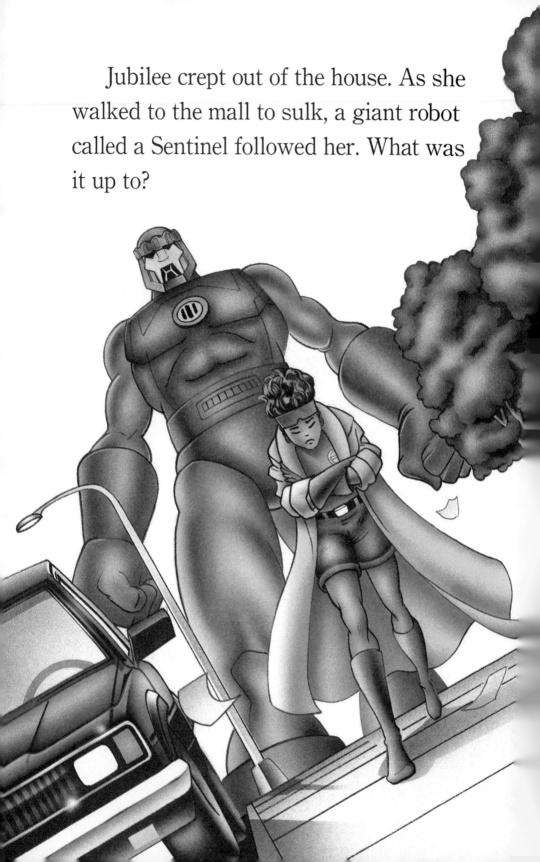

Jubilee went to the arcade. But her hurt and anger at her parents made her plasma energy go crazy. It shot through her fingertips and into the arcade game. The machine exploded!

Jubilee ran out of the arcade and slammed into two shoppers. They were Storm and Rogue—and they were mutants, too! "What's your hurry, sugar?" said Rogue.

Suddenly the Sentinel came crashing
through the mall's glass walls. The robot
found Jubilee—and grabbed her.

"Hey! Put me down!" screamed Jubilee.

Storm flew to the rescue and freed Jubilee.

Then Rogue took over. She threw the robot across the mall!

"Did you see that?" gasped Jubilee.

"Rogue has a way with men," said Storm.

Gambit, another mutant, appeared. He flicked his charged cards at the robot while Jubilee hid behind him.

The Sentinel was up again. It threw a ball of knockout gas at Jubilee. She tried to run. But she was choking!

Then the mutant Cyclops appeared. He caught Jubilee—and blasted off the Sentinel's head!

It was too much for Jubilee. She fainted, and everything went black.

When Jubilee finally woke up, she was in a strange bed.

"Where am I? What is this place?" she said.

But no one answered. She began to explore.

She walked down the long hallways, peeking into room after room. In one, she saw a mutant called Beast. He was holding up a test tube.

Moving on, she saw another mutant
watching a senator on TV. His name was
Morph. He kept changing form!

To the senator…

and back to Morph again.

What a strange man! Jubilee thought.

Professor X, the leader of the mutant
band known as the X-Men, was in his office
with Jean Grey, who had telepathic powers.

Suddenly she sensed that Jubilee was
on the loose.

"The girl! She's gone!" said Jean.

They set off the alarm.

Jubilee ran into a room. The door slammed shut behind her. She was locked in. The room pulsed with bright lights and strange noises. Then she saw Gambit, who was being attacked by a fierce mutant with *claws!*

Gambit had rescued Jubilee at the mall. Now she came to Gambit's rescue. She knocked down the clawed mutant with a blast of plasma.

Just then the doors slid open. The other X-Men stood there staring. Their teammate Wolverine, the clawed mutant, had been knocked down by a gutsy teen!

The X-Men laughed. But Wolverine didn't think it was so funny!

"What *is* this weird place?" Jubilee asked.

Beast answered her.

"It's called the Danger Room. It's part gym, part survival course. We learn self-defense in here."

"Come with me, Jubilee," said Storm. "I'll explain everything to you."

Storm and Jubilee went up to the roof to talk.

"Everyone here is a mutant, just like you," said Storm. "Professor Xavier is our leader. He has named us the X-Men. This place is Professor Xavier's School for Gifted Youngsters.

"Here we learn to control our mutant powers for the benefit of all. I can command the weather, so they call me Storm."

"Why does everyone hate us?" asked Jubilee.

"People fear what they don't understand," said Storm.

Later, Professor X called the X-Men
into the War Room.

"I found a photo of Jubilee in the
computer bank of the robot from the mall,"
he said. "This photo comes from the
Mutant Control Agency in Washington.
That's how the Sentinel found her!"

"Is the government plotting against us?" said Cyclops.

"Not the government," said Professor X. "But someone *inside* the government!"

"The Mutant Control Agency has files," said Professor X. "Those files hold the names of hundreds of innocent mutants. Someone in the agency fooled them into giving up their names. We are *all* in terrible danger!"

Wolverine spoke next.

"So we get the files, and we shred them!"

Just then Jean rushed into the War Room.

"Jubilee has run away!" she cried.

But there was no time to rescue one mutant. Hundreds were in danger! Professor X had a plan, but the X-Men had to act quickly!

2
The Break-in

Storm, Rogue, Wolverine, Beast, and Morph flew in their jet, the Blackbird, to the Mutant Control Agency headquarters. Cyclops was in command.

First Wolverine used his claws to tear open the door. "Just like a can of tuna!" he said.

Beast shut off the alarm system.

"Here are the files!" cried Storm. The X-Men ripped them apart. They were ready to leave…but it wasn't going to be so easy.

Armed guards were swarming everywhere. Sentinels loomed over the X-Men. Wolverine rushed at a Sentinel.

"Hey, tin man, I'm sending you back to Oz," he said. "In pieces!"

A Sentinel began firing at Wolverine. Morph quickly jumped in front of

Wolverine to protect him.

"Look out, Wolverine!" he screamed.

Back at headquarters, Jean and Professor X cried out. They sensed what had happened.

"Morph is...*dead!*" gasped Jean.

The X-Men ran for the Blackbird. On the way, Beast got caught in an electric fence. And where was Morph? Nobody knew.

"We have to go back to the school," said Cyclops. "We can't risk any more lives!"

But Wolverine had other ideas.

"I'm going back for Beast and Morph," he said. "The X-Men don't run. They stay and fight!"

Cyclops gave a signal to Rogue. Rogue could drain anyone of his power with a touch of her hand. She touched Wolverine…and he slumped to the ground.

"Morph, Beast!" he cried weakly.

Cyclops got everyone on the jet. "Being an X-Man is not easy. But teamwork is still the best way."

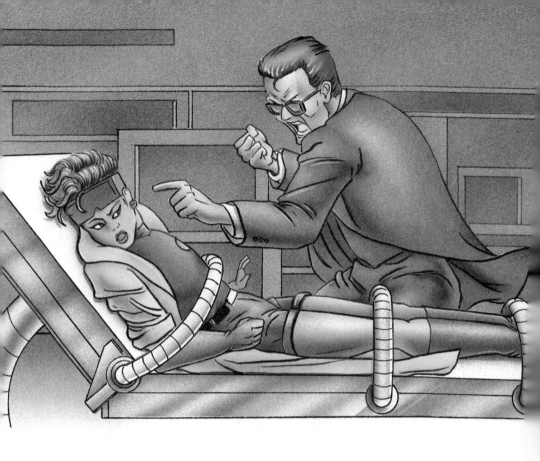

Meanwhile, where was Jubilee? After her escape from the school, she had tried to run home. But she was captured by Sentinels. She was now in a far-off city, the prisoner of a man named Henry Peter Gyrich. He had taken her to his hideout in an old warehouse.

He was firing commands at her.

"Our Mutant Control registration files have been destroyed," he growled. "Give me the names of other mutants! Names! I want names!"

"I don't know anything!" cried Jubilee. "I want to go home! I'm just a kid!"

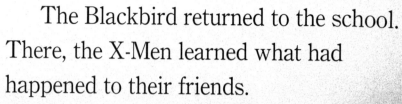

The Blackbird returned to the school.
There, the X-Men learned what had
happened to their friends.

"Beast is in jail," said Jean.

"And Morph...Morph is dead,"
said Professor X.

"I'll avenge you, friends!" cried Wolverine. He stormed out.

"I know you feel bad," Cyclops called after him. "It's not your fault!"

But Wolverine was gone. He wanted to be alone with his pain.

3
The Showdown

In the War Room, the X-Men watched the news on TV. The president was speaking.

"Experimental robot policemen called Sentinels stopped an attack by mutants at the Mutant Control Agency here in Washington," she said.

As Cyclops watched, he formed a plan to discover the whereabouts of the Sentinels' secret base. But the plan needed teamwork.

Cyclops finally found Wolverine in a pool hall.

"If you came to apologize for leaving Beast and Morph, save it," growled Wolverine.

"I never apologize for making command decisions," said Cyclops. "But how would you like to find the Sentinels' home base?"

Wolverine smiled wickedly.

"When and where?" he asked.

That evening, the president sent for Gyrich.

"I want you to shut down the Mutant Registration Program," she said firmly. "Those mutants risked their lives to destroy those files. They must have reason to be afraid."

Gyrich was *furious*. When he left the Oval Office, his cellular phone rang. It was Jubilee's father. Cyclops was at his house!

"One of the mutants is here!" said Jubilee's father. He didn't know Gyrich was holding his daughter prisoner.

"Keep him there," said Gyrich.

And he sent a Sentinel to capture Cyclops.

As Cyclops left the house, the Sentinel stopped him.

"Surrender, mutant!" it said.

"Of course…*not!*" said Cyclops. He lifted his sunglasses and aimed an optic blast right at the Sentinel.

Crash! The Sentinel's arm fell off!

It flew off to its home base for repair.
Nearby, Storm was watching. The
Blackbird took off after the Sentinel.
Cyclops's plan was working like a charm!

The broken Sentinel crash-landed at the Sentinel base. Its landing damaged the base, cutting off all power!

Instantly, Jubilee's electric bonds came off. She was free!

"All *right!* I'm out of here!" she said,
and blasted out—straight through the
wall.

Jubilee found herself surrounded by
Sentinels. She fell to her knees.

"I just want to go home!" she cried.

Cyclops appeared.

"Jubilee—duck!" he yelled.

Gambit charged in and rescued Jubilee.

"Did you miss me?" he said.

"Did I ever!" said Jubilee.

Storm zapped a Sentinel with a bolt of lightning. Rogue smashed one into scrap metal!

Wolverine got the last Sentinel. He dug his claws into its neck.

"This one's for you, Morph!" he cried.

Ruined Sentinels lay everywhere.
Gyrich was gone.

"We did it. We got them all," said
Cyclops.

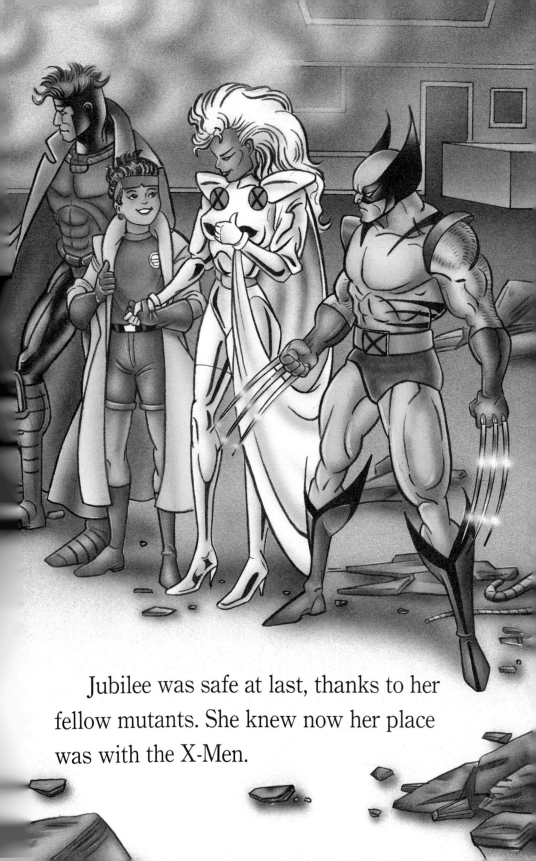

Jubilee was safe at last, thanks to her
fellow mutants. She knew now her place
was with the X-Men.

It was time for Jubilee to say good-bye to her foster parents.

"Professor Xavier's school is the best place for me," she said. "I will be with the

other X-Men. And I will learn to use my mutant powers for the benefit of everybody."

Jubilee's foster parents understood. They hugged Jubilee with tears in their eyes.

"Will you come back and visit?" said Jubilee's mother.

"Does a mall babe eat chili fries?" asked Jubilee with a wink.